Copyright© 2020, Linda K. Bridges
Critter Creations
PO Box 62903
Colorado Springs, CO 80962

Website: https://www.lindakbridges.com/hildies-hat-party/

All rights and international rights reserved. No part of this product, including but not limited to cards and guidebook or any portion thereof may be reproduced, distributed, or transmitted in any form or by any means, including photocopying, recording, or other electronic or mechanical methods, nor may it be stored in a retrieval system, transmitted or otherwise copied for public or private use, without the prior written permission of the publisher, except in the case of "fair use" of brief quotations embodied in critical reviews and certain other noncommercial uses permitted by copyright law. For permission requests, write to the publisher, addressed "Attention: Permissions Coordinator," at the address above.

The intent of the authors is only to offer information of a general nature to help you in your quest for overall well-being. In the event you use any of the information in this book for yourself, which is your constitutional right, the authors and the publisher assume no responsibility for your actions.

First Printing, 2020
ISBN 978-1-734-8491-0-3
Library of Congress Control Number: ZXXXXX

1. JUV002000   JUVENILE FICTION / Animals / General
2. JUV010000   JUVENILE FICTION / Bedtime & Dreams
3. JUV039060   JUVENILE FICTION / Social Themes / Friendship

Written and illustrated by Linda K. Bridges

For information about this book, or to order copies, please contact:

Critter Creations
PO Box 62903, Colorado Springs, CO 80962
Website: https://www.lindakbridges.com/hildies-hat-party/

PRINTED IN CHINA
10 9 8 7 6   5 4 3 2 1

To every child who loves a good party.

To my beloved grandchildren.
You were my inspiration for writing and illustrating this book,
because of your love of reading and your innate curiosity about
all God's critters, great and small.

Thanks to my son, Jared, for his artistic layout design and
graphic skills that made this book come alive on the paper,
and my numerous friends and colleagues for encouraging me to
get this story finished. I am forever grateful
for your loving and helpful advice.

And many thanks to my husband, Al. I could have never pushed
through to the end without your faith in me.

THIS BOOK BELONGS TO:

Enjoy the Party!
Linda K. Bridges
2020

HILDIE'S HAT PARTY

written and illustrated by
Linda K. Bridges

Hildie Hedgehog threw open her bedroom window.

The morning air smelled sweet as honeysuckle and was as warm as a sunlit pond.

Spring had come to the Big Woods!

The Flower Fairies had come in the night, spreading their magic all around.

Flowers bloomed everywhere.

Hildie clapped with delight.

Hildie tucked one into a cluster of snow bells, hoping the Flower Fairies would come to the party, too.

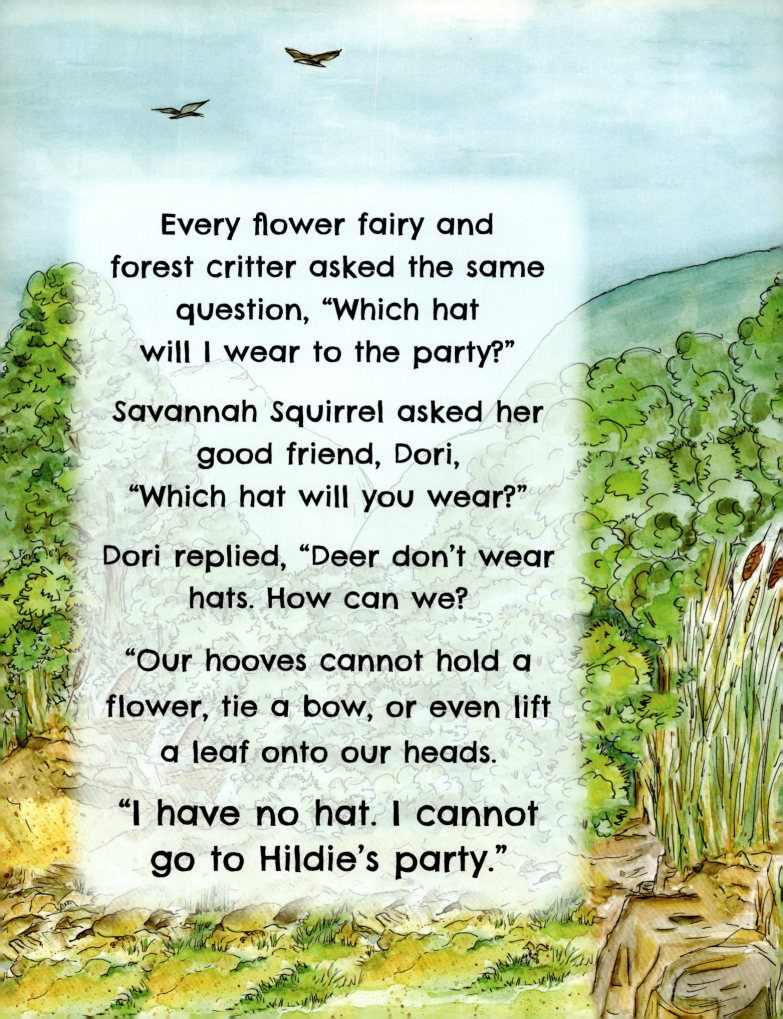

Every flower fairy and forest critter asked the same question, "Which hat will I wear to the party?"

Savannah Squirrel asked her good friend, Dori, "Which hat will you wear?"

Dori replied, "Deer don't wear hats. How can we?

"Our hooves cannot hold a flower, tie a bow, or even lift a leaf onto our heads.

"I have no hat. I cannot go to Hildie's party."

Dori blinked back her tears and walked into the woods alone.

The news about Dori's problem traveled quickly through Big Woods.

Everyone arrived at Hildie's den.

"Dori doesn't want to come to your party if she can't wear a hat," squeaked Mouse.

"Wearing a hat is fun, but it's not the most important thing," replied Hildie.

"My party is for us to sing and dance with our friends, and to celebrate the coming of spring."

The critters croaked, quacked and squeaked their agreement.

Before anyone could say, "THE BEAVERS ARE BUILDING A DAM,"

Hildie dashed inside her den and returned pulling a cart loaded with hats.

"My mama always said, 'Hildie, when you have a big problem, put on your thinking hat. Then your problem will soon be solved!'"

Each animal grabbed a hat.

Quiet settled over the circle of friends.

Thinking.

Thinking.

Thinking.

The only sound heard was a rustling leaf when someone wiggled.

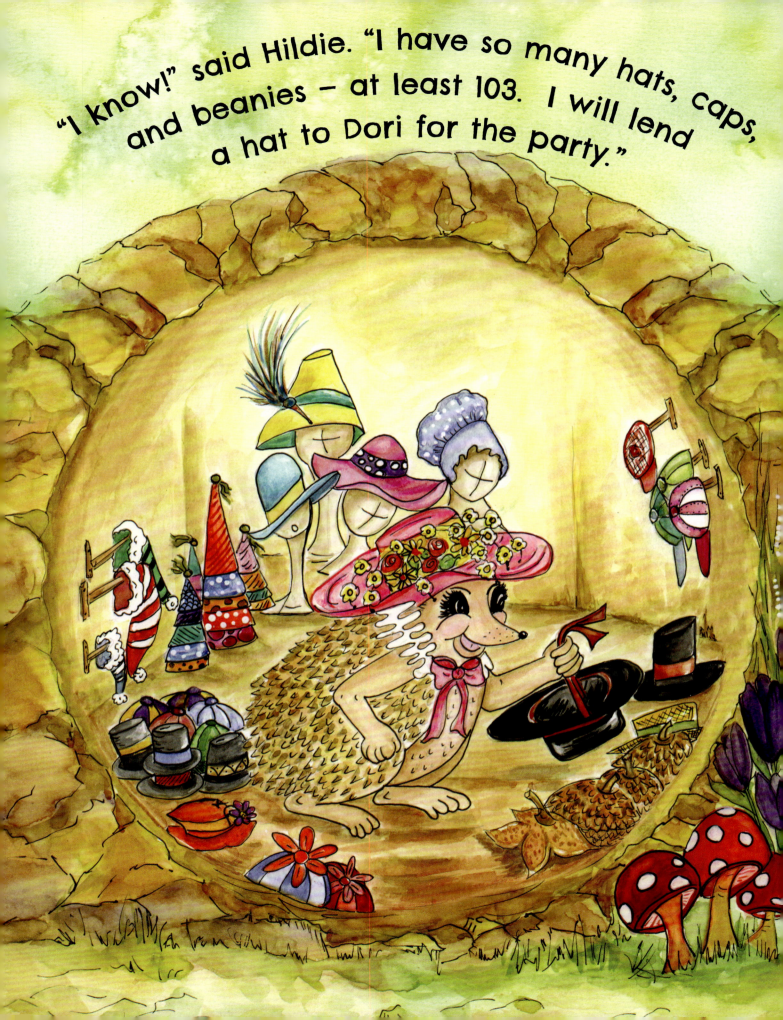

"Hoot-
hoot-
a-hoo,"
said
Mr. Owl.

"That is a brilliant idea, Hildie!
And those of us with paws or claws
can lift the hat onto her head."

Soon everyone was chattering about their ideas.

"WAHOO!" whooped Hildie, tossing her hat into the air.

"Let's go tell Dori!"

The critters threw their thinking hats into the air, too.

They clapped, honked, croaked and tweeted.

Mr. Owl made his very owlish, "Hoot-hoot-a-hoo!"

Before anyone could say,

"THE SQUIRRELS ARE HOARDING THEIR NUTS,"

the critters were on their way to the quiet cove where Dori lived.

The band of critters arrived just as the little deer woke from her nap.

"Dori! Each of us has brought something to make a hat for you to wear to my party," said Hildie.

Everyone worked together to make Dori's Hat.

Dori DANCED and PRANCED for joy.

Now she could go to Hildie's party!

A colorful band of forest critters gathered near the pond.

They danced and played until the moon and stars rose high in the sky.

Hildie smiled.

Spring had come at last.

Conversation Starters

What did Hildie like most about the coming of Spring?

Why didn't Dori Deer want to come to Hildie's party?

What big idea did Hildie Hedgehog have to solve Dori Deer's problem?

Why did the forest friends want to help Dori?

What could you do to help a friend who might not be able to come to a party?

ABOUT THE AUTHOR

Linda K. Bridges was born and raised in Bakersfield, California. She and her husband lived in Vienna, Austria for 15 years before returning to the United States.
After their kids were grown they spent 5 years in Thailand. Together they raised four children and now have nine grandchildren.

Linda describes herself as a late-bloomer in the field of writing and illustrating children's storybooks, but nevertheless believes deeply that it's never too late to pursue your dreams. HILDIE'S HAT PARTY is her second book.

Linda lives with her husband and their serendipitous critter, Sherlock (a miniature schnauzer), in Colorado Springs, Colorado.

You can follow Linda at WWW.LINDAKBRIDGES.COM to see what else she is working on.